Shō and the Demons of the Deep

cf

Shō and the
Demons of the Deep

written and painted
by Annouchka Gravel Galouchko

Annick Press Ltd.
Toronto • New York

THE CANADA COUNCIL | LE CONSEIL DES ARTS
FOR THE ARTS | DU CANADA
SINCE 1957 | DEPUIS 1957

Annick Press gratefully acknowledges the support of the
Canada Council and the Ontario Arts Council.

Translated by Stéphan Daigle.

Cataloguing in Publication Data

Gravel Galouchko, Annouchka, 1960-
  [Sho et les dragons d'eau.   English]
  Sho and the demons of the deep

Translation of: Sho et les dragons d'eau.
ISBN 1-55037-398-6 (bound) ISBN 1-55037-393-5 (pbk.)

I. Title. II. Title: Sho et les dragons d'eau. English.

PS8563.R39158.S5613   jC843'.54   C95-930878-4
PZ7.G35Sh

The art in this book was rendered in gouache.
The text was typeset in President.

Distributed in Canada by: Published in the U.S.A. by Annick Press (U.S.) Ltd.
Firefly Books Ltd.   Distributed in the U.S.A. by:
3680 Victoria Park Avenue Firefly Books (U.S.) Inc.
Willowdale, ON   P.O. Box 1338
M2H 3K1   Ellicott Station
                           Buffalo, NY 14205

Printed on acid-free paper.

Printed and bound in Canada by
Friesens, Altona, Manitoba.

This book is a tribute to
Hokusai, who was a guide
and inspiration for my inner journey.

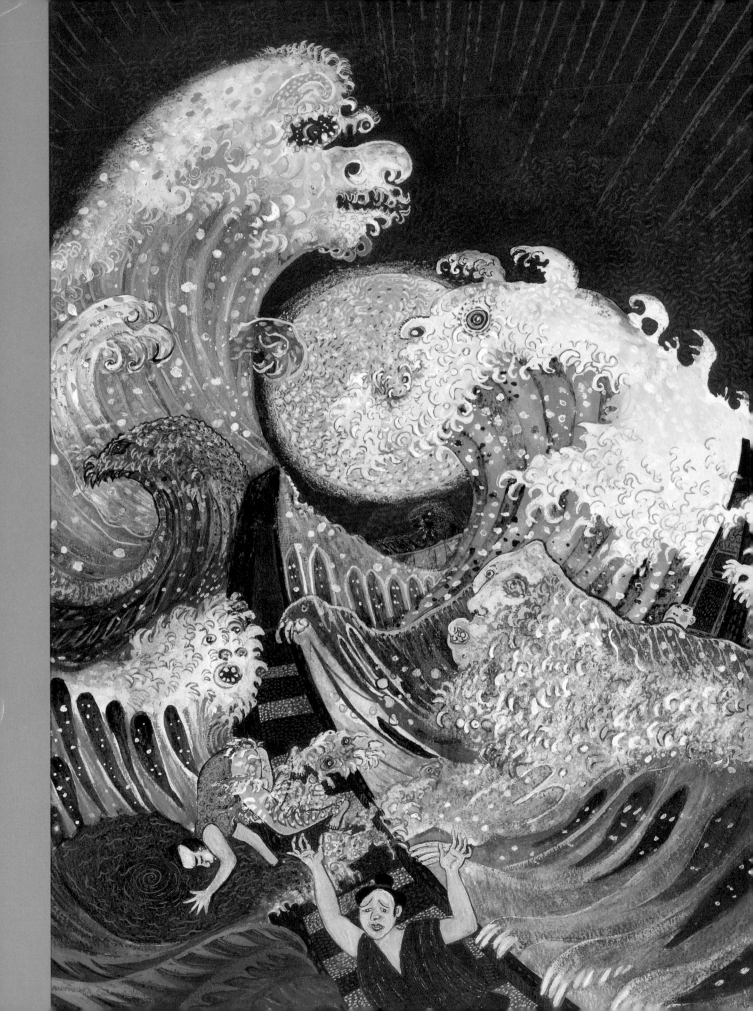

It is said that in ancient Japan people cast their nightmares into the sea. These folk were too shy to reveal their secret dreams, and so they put them in bags and set them adrift on the waves.

The sea felt burdened by people's sorrows. Softened by the water, the bags would open and the nightmares would spill out and escape like little demons. In the end there were so many that the sea became quite disturbed, and monstrous waves lashed the shores, attacking the fishermen peacefully fishing in their small boats. Some men disappeared forever, and fishing became too dangerous. The market stalls that used to teem with fresh fish each morning were now bare. Fish became rare and expensive to buy, and only the emperor and other rich people could afford it.

In a village near the ocean, a wealthy family employed a little girl to tend their garden. Her fisherman father had lost his livelihood because of the demon waves.

Shō had the rare gift of looking into the hearts of all living things, and even inside the rocks and the stones, the moon and the stars. One summer evening two fishermen came to her and said, "Our situation is desperate. The ocean has turned against us. Demons fill the sea and the villagers are starving. We are even afraid to go near the water to collect mussels and seaweed for soup."

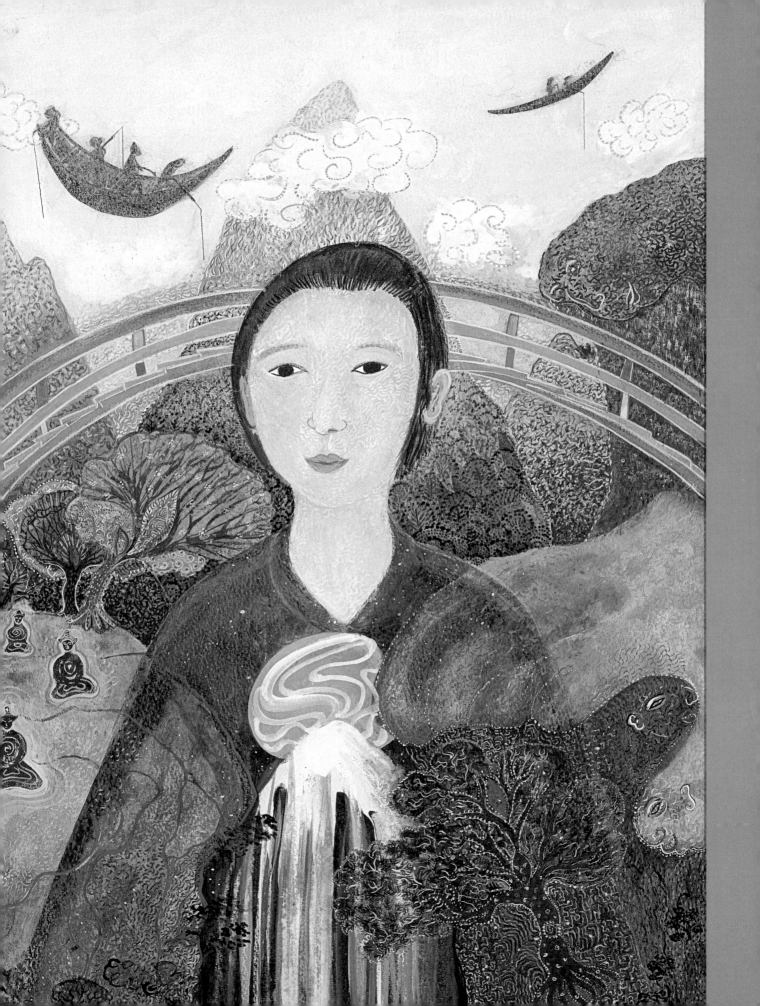

Shō listened and finally said, "Together we can overcome this calamity, but we must follow three conditions. First, you must promise to give a week's catch of fish to the poor once you return to your work; second, I will go out to sea, but you must accompany me and stay to the end, no matter what happens; and third, please persuade the people to stop casting their nightmares into the waters." The fishermen agreed.

At midnight they met at the shore and boarded the small fishing vessel. They put out to sea. The moon was full and silvery waves were licking the sides of the boat. The sea was calm, the demon waves asleep. The coastline lay peaceful in the moonlight.

Shō rose and called the waves to her like birds to a feeding hand. "Come on now, come on out…" she sang with her gentle voice. No sooner had she finished than the demon waves arrived like a giant explosion around the boat, riding crests, spewing foam. The fishermen desperately clung to the sides of the boat, but Shō stayed so calm that they were ashamed of themselves.

"My little dragons," she began, "you are but foam and bubbles on the waves, soon to be burst by the playful winds." The child's soothing voice melted all their fury and the demons disappeared, just as she had predicted. The waters were calm once again and the four brave souls returned safely to port.

The fishermen fulfilled the third condition and spoke to all the villagers about the bad effect the nightmares were having on the sea that fed them all. And the people promised to stop throwing bad dreams into the ocean.

Prosperity returned, the markets filled with fish, the fishermen gave a week's catch to the poor, and Shō returned to school.

The village enjoyed harmony for a while, but soon it became clear that people were hiding secrets. Their closets were overflowing with nightmares hidden there in bags. What were they going to do?

One day soon a strange and sombre figure arrived, pushing a large cart in front of him. He began knocking on doors, representing himself as the refuse collector in the emperor's employ. He offered to dispose of the offending bags—for a price. He charged one silver coin per bag, two for the heavier ones. The people were so eager to get rid of their secrets that they agreed to pay.

The man filled his pockets—and at night dumped the bags into the ocean. Soon the watery tempest started once more. The demon waves spread terror among the villagers, but the man had disappeared.

When Shō was called once again, she realized that she had to teach the sea how to banish the demons.

In the early morning light she stood on the beach and addressed the ocean: "You must defend yourself. At high tide you must charge with your mightiest waves and spew the demons back onto the shore. Don't be afraid, or you will never be free of them."

There was no response. The sea remained calm and Shō went home.

But at noon there arose such a thunderous growl, such howling of wind and rolling of waves, that all the villagers came running, and watched from the top of the cliffs. In one giant monstrous thrust, the sea threw all the demons out, and only a green sludge remained on the beach. The people cheered and danced and praised Shō and the ocean who had saved them once more.

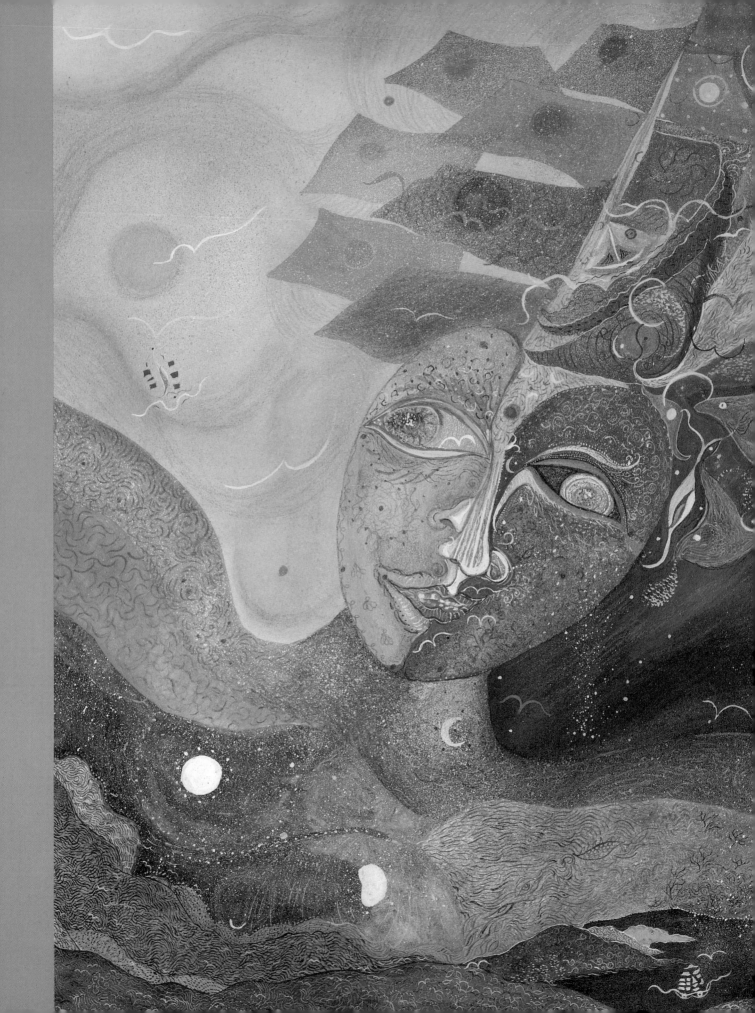

Finally the ocean was able to breathe again. Dolphins jumped playfully from the waves and birds were singing everywhere. The forests and mountains shone in a new light.

The children were the first to ask Shō her secret, so she taught them to play with their bad dreams rather than fear them: instead of casting them into the sea, they were to toss them into the air. The dreams would thrive on light.

One young boy drew pictures of his dreams, then began to cut shapes out of them and paint them all the colours of the rainbow. Soon other children followed his example, and they painted cats' and dragons' faces on their cut-outs and tossed them up to the winds.

When the parents saw the children playing with images of their fears and enjoying themselves, they joined the children with drawings of their own. One glued a light frame of wood onto the paper and attached a long string. He offered his dreams to the wind, and this time they rose and danced and remained aloft, controlled by the string in his hand. People all around, hypnotized by this vision of light and colour floating in the sky, discovered the first kite.

Since that time there have been yearly festivals to celebrate the kite all around the world. Children and adults still build their own kites together and send them soaring into the sun and wind.

ANNOUCHKA GRAVEL GALOUCHKO

Fifteen years ago, Annouchka was travelling the roads of North America with her flute. Those passersby who stopped to throw a few coins into her hat found their hearts beginning to dance.

Magic, dreams and fantasy always intersect; the language of goblins and spirits, the same that has shaped the stories of all lands, is the language of Annouchka's art. Whether she holds paintbrush, pencil or flute, enchantment awaits us.